Harry The Happy Mouse

n.g.k.

Illustrated by Janelle Dimmett

www.ngkmedia.com
www.harrythehappymouse.com

Instagram @ngk.author
Etsy Store: etsy.harrythehappymouse.com

1st Edition (Special Edition)

Katie and Harry's Bridge

The Sugar Mill

Katie's Cake Shop

Bat's Tree

The
Harry The
Happy Mouse
Series

Frog's Log

The Pumpkin Patch

READERS' FAVORITE
FIVE STARS

Mole's House

The Flour Mill

The Family Home

On the crest of a wave, and the wisp of the wind,

Harry the Happy Mouse was thinking good things.

Under a bridge, he lived with his wife,
What a lovely day, "Wow, this is the life!"

Every summer's evening, after something to eat,
He strolled along the stream, to see who he'd meet.

The frogs they did croak, and the birds they did tweet,
The dogs they did bark and the sheep they did bleat!

Across the stream...

...with a step and a jump.

An extra long leap to get over a bump!

Harry's favourite part of his long summer walks,
Was meeting other animals and having long talks.

One sunny evening, whilst walking along,
   He found a sad Frog, who was stuck on a log!

"Help me, I'm stuck!" the Frog shouted down.
   "Quickly Happy Mouse! I don't want to drown!

When I jumped up it didn't look high,
   Now I'm up here, right up in the sky!"

Quick as a flash, Harry climbed to the top,
   Brave as can be, no thought of the drop!

"Look here dear Frog, climb on my back,
   I'll get us back down, back down on the track."

Harry climbed down, the Frog jumped with glee,
"Thank you, kind Mouse, for rescuing me!"

"You shouldn't thank me, just help someone too!
    That'll be better, for me and for you!"

"But why?" said the Frog, "That doesn't help you?
    If I help someone else, then who will help you?!"

"When you help someone else, it makes you feel grand!
    So, when someone needs help, just give them a hand!"

"Thank you, kind Mouse, you've made my day,
    and if you don't mind, I'll be on my way!"

Whilst hopping back home to his green lily pad,
  The Frog saw a Mole, who was looking quite sad.

"What's wrong?" asked the Frog, "Why the big frown?"
  "This hole" said the Mole, "My son's fallen down!"

"Oh dear!" said the Frog, "Now what can we do?
  Don't worry Mrs. Mole, I will help you!"

The Frog found a stick, and the Mole found some string,
They made a great fishing rod to pull out the young thing.

Baby Mole climbed out, and his Mum jumped with glee!
"Thank you, kind Frog, for rescuing me!"

"You shouldn't thank me, just help someone too!
That'll be better, for me and for you!"

"But why?" said the Mole, "That doesn't help you?
If I help someone else, then who will help you?!"

"When you help someone else, it makes you feel grand!
So, when someone needs help, just give them a hand!"

The Mole carried on with her son in tow,
The moonlight twinkled with a beautiful glow.

"Quickly young man, you should be in bed."
The Mole said to her son, whilst resting his head.

"But wait!" said the Mole, "Whatever is that?"
Upside down in a tree hung a very grumpy Bat.

"Excuse me Mr. Bat, why are you sad?
Whatever it is, it can't be that bad!"

"It is!" said the Bat, with a cry and a quiver,
"It's my hat you see, it fell in the river!"

"Oh no!" said the Mole, "It looks like it's stuck,
We'll get it back, with a plan and some luck."

"Thanks!" said the Bat, "But what can we do?
It's way too far down, for me and for you!"

The Mole said, "I'll hold my son, and you hold me,
    We can't do it with one, but we might with three!"

The Mole held her son and she held the Bat,
    Before they knew it, they'd rescued the hat.

"What a great plan!" the Bat jumped with glee!
    "Thank you, kind Mole, for rescuing it for me!"

"You shouldn't thank me, just help someone too!
    That'll be better, for me and for you!"

"But why?" said the Bat, "That doesn't help you?
    If I help someone else, then who will help you?!"

"When you help someone else, it makes you feel grand!
    So when someone needs help, just give them a hand!"

"Very well." said the Bat, "I'll make sure I do,
    Goodnight, Mrs. Mole, and to your son too!"

Everyone's sleeping,
            so cosy and snug,
The cows, the birds,
            and even the bugs.

The very next day, Harry got home from his walk,
But Harry was sad, not happy, not glad!

"What's wrong?" asked his wife, "Why the big frown?
You're normally so happy, but now you seem down."

"There's no one to help." said Harry the Mouse.
"Not a frog, not a cat, not a mole, nor a grouse!"

"When I help someone else, it makes me feel grand,
When there's no one to help, I can't lend a hand!"

Harry's wife said "Come here, I have a surprise,
　　Because you're so helpful, so kind and so wise!"

"You see Harry, that Frog you helped, well...

...he helped a Mole...

...and also, a Cat."

"She helped a Dog, and also a Rat!"

"The Dog helped an Owl, and the Owl helped a Bird!"

"The Bird helped a Cow, in fact, the whole herd!"

"Now everyone's here, just to see you,
The Frog, the Mole and the Bat too!

All this kindness is spreading you see,
Now we're all happy, as happy as can be!"

"Wow!" said Harry, "Look what I've done!
I started all this by just helping one!"

On the crest of a wave, and the wisp of the wind,

Harry the Happy Mouse had done wonderful things.

Books by N.G.K.

harrythehappymouse.com

Walter The Worlds Worst Pirate

Book 1

Harry's Lovely Spring Day

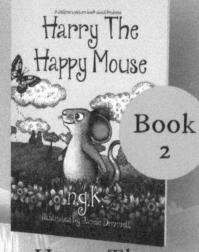

Book 2

Harry The Happy Mouse

Book 3

Harry's Spooky Surprise!

Book 4

Harry The Christmas Mouse

Book 5

Harry Saves The Ocean!

For ages 7-10

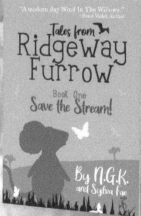

Tales From Ridgeway Furrow

Lightning Source UK Ltd.
Milton Keynes UK
UKHW021635150322
400080UK00005B/81